Sage's Big Adventure:
Living with Blindness

Sage's Big Adventure:
Living with Blindness

To Ivy —
Enjoy Sage's story!

Sage

Gayle M. Irwin

Gayle M. Irwin
5/13/08

To order additional copies of this book, contact:
Xlibris Corporation
1-888-795-4274
www.Xlibris.com
Orders@Xlibris.com
39077

CONTENTS

This Story is Dedicated . . .

To God's creatures, human and animal—
whose courage, dedication and faith inspire us.

To the children of the earth—
no matter how tough life gets,
keep your spirit filled and alive with faith and hope.
Go forth and let your light shine!

To the Eternal God and Great Creator—
the wonders you have made, the blessings you continually give,
the talents and gifts you bestow
are priceless and immeasurable.

To Sage, my friend and companion;
To my many beloved friends;
and
to my loving and precious family.

Special Thanks . . .

To God, the Great Creator—
for all His great gifts,
especially His beautiful creations,
His gentle whisper, and His eternal love!

To my husband and my parents—
your love, encouragement and commitment
are among my richest and most inspirational blessings!

To my dear friends,
many of whom shared thoughts and comments on this book—
the time you gave, the input you provided,
and the sincere friendship, advice and guidance you offer:
for all this and more, I am truly grateful!

To Sage, a beautiful Creation of God—
You inspired this book;
your blindness does not stop you from living and loving;
your "go-for-it" attitude and strong, loving heart
are a marvel and a beauty to behold, sweet dog!

My Prayer . . .

May the children of today
always find positive inspiration
and grow into the heroes and hope-keepers of tomorrow.

May the adults of this world
never extinguish the wondrous light of children,
crush their hope,
or destroy their awesome and glorious spirit.

May all people have the courage and insight
to listen to the Great Creator
when He whispers.

Gayle M. Irwin

CHAPTER 1

A Dog Named Sage

Not long ago at a small house with a backyard filled with bright green grass lived a dog named Sage. She was white with many large black spots, and even some small ones! Her fur was wavy, even on her tail. Sage was a Springer Spaniel, a type of dog that loves to smell, listen, look for, and find birds.

Like many Springer Spaniels, Sage wanted to explore, but she had a difficult time walking, playing, and discovering. You see, she also had a secret—she could not see. Sage was blind.

Even when she was a puppy Sage's eyes did not see well. She soon realized that she was different from her brothers and sisters; they ran and played without fear. She wanted to run but when she did she stumbled and bumped into things. So, she walked and listened and sniffed. Within a few months, she knew her way around the house and the yard by using her senses of hearing and smell. She listened to the many sounds, such as birds singing and airplanes flying overhead. Her ears even picked up some sounds the humans of the house could not hear. She sniffed the air and every corner of the little house and the backyard. Soon, Sage, too, was active both inside and outside.

The little pup spent many hours in the yard with her mother and her brothers and sisters. Sometimes she slept, curled up on the thick grass in the warm summer sun. Other times she played. She chewed on toy bones. She rolled around and wrestled with her four brothers and two sisters. If they ran to another part of the yard, Sage stood still and listened; she could find where they were by following their yips and yelps. If she bumped into things, including her brothers and sisters or the children of the humans she lived with, people said she was just being a wobbly, exploring puppy. They did not know Sage's secret.

Sage's sense of smell was keen. She not only listened to her brothers and sisters, she tracked them by putting her nose to the ground and following their different scents. She also discovered other animals this way, such as robins and rabbits. She wanted to play with these creatures, but they never stayed around long enough to enjoy a game with her.

When she smelled or heard another animal, Sage became excited, wagging her tail and turning her head toward whatever she heard or smelled. That's why no one knew Sage was blind, even as she grew into an adult dog.

CHAPTER 2

Moving to a New Home

When she was two years old, a new family came to the house and took Sage to their home many miles away. This family had no children, and they wanted a pretty and active dog to live with them.

On the way to her new home, Sage sat in the back seat of the car. She listened and she sniffed. Sometimes her body trembled. This new car with new people made her feel confused and a little frightened.

Where was she going in this strange car? Where were the people and the home she knew so well? Where was her mother? Sage wanted to be where things were familiar. What was going to happen to her and how could she get along in a different place with people she did not know?

Upon arrival at her new home, the man helped Sage from the car. He set her on the sidewalk, and Sage obediently followed him by listening to the sounds of his voice and his footsteps. Suddenly, Sage's front legs bumped into something hard. She immediately stopped walking. She stretched her body and sniffed the air. No strange smell came to her, only the scent of the man and woman who stood beside her. Sage was confused.

She heard the man gently say, "Come, Sage."

But the young dog did not know where to put her feet. She wondered if a brick wall was in front of her.

Sage felt a tug on her leash, and the man's voice again said, "Come, Sage."

The dog carefully stretched out her right front foot. She felt solid ground, so she set her foot down then put her left front foot forward.

Again, the man said, "Come, Sage!"

Sage carefully placed first one front foot forward, then the next. Finding something solid to stand on, she carefully continued up three more stairs.

"She seems afraid of stairs," the woman said softly.

As the man led Sage through the house, the dog's nose picked up the scents of these people throughout all the rooms.

"This is going to be your new home, Sage," the woman said. "We want to become good friends and do many fun things together. There's a big backyard here for you to play in. Let's go see it!"

Sage heard a large door open then a smaller one. She felt another tug on her leash. She followed her new family by listening to their footsteps. She stopped quickly when she felt a slant to the floor and a drop-off in front of her.

"Come on, Sage," the man said. "It's okay."

Still Sage did not move. She was scared! What had happened to the ground? She couldn't feel it when she stretched her paw out in front of her body.

"She really does seem afraid of stairs," the woman said again.

"But didn't her former owners have stairs on their back porch?" the husband asked.

"Yes, they did, and I saw her take those just fine," the woman answered.

"Come, Sage," the man said firmly.

Instead, Sage lay on the floor, fearful of what he wanted her to do. Then she felt him move her body, pick up her paws and move them out and then down. Sage trembled. But, the man still moved her front paws downward.

Her feet touched something solid. Sage inched her body forward, raised herself up and took a few cautious steps forward. Her feet felt the ground, and then she brought her entire body out of the doorway. She smelled fresh air, and she breathed deeply.

"I wonder if she has a balance problem," the woman said quietly. "I remember her other owners saying she was skittish around loud noises.

"Perhaps," the woman added thoughtfully, "someone set off a firecracker too close to her ears, and that causes her to be off balance, especially with stairs."

"I suppose that's possible," the man replied.

"When we take her in for her shots, let's ask the doctor to check her ears and her balance."

"Good idea," the man said.

Sage heard the snap of the leash and felt it being removed from her collar. "Go explore your new yard, girl," the man said to her.

Sage took a few hesitant steps forward. She stood on a concrete porch in the springtime sun. Sage felt the warmth on her fur and smelled the crisp afternoon air. She took a deep breath. Instead of smelling a place filled with strange scents, her nose detected clean fresh air and other outdoor fragrances.

She felt a bit more comfortable because this is what she liked—being outdoors in the fresh air and sunshine! Momentarily forgetting she was in a new place, Sage joyfully leaped into the air then began to run.

Suddenly, her head hit something hard, and Sage tumbled down. She lay on the ground and heard the man and woman quickly come to her. Sage stood up on wobbly legs and then shook herself.

"Sage! Are you all right?!" the woman asked anxiously.

"Goodness! She hit that tree hard," the man said.

"Something *is* wrong with her!" said the woman.

"She's confused," her husband replied. "This is her first day with us. Give her some time to adjust."

However, Sage's experiences at her new home during the next few days did not get better.

CHAPTER 3

Living with Blindness

One day while her people were gone, Sage was lying on the living room sofa. She heard loud noises outside the house near the backyard. Sage sat up and turned her head, listening and trying to understand what was making the noise. She heard two strange male voices. Then she heard pounding on the outside wall of the house. Sage barked loudly in warning, and momentarily the noises stopped. Then the pounding, like a hammer against the wall, continued and grew louder.

The men's voices were also loud as they shouted to each other.

"Right here!" one of the men yelled. "The wire goes here."

A small machine began to drill into the wall. Sage jumped from the sofa in fright. She barked again, two sharp *WHOOFS,* and growled deep in her throat, but the noises did not stop.

Frightened, Sage jumped from the sofa and tried to find a way out of the house, but she couldn't find an open door. She barked again, this time with fear and then ran around the room in confusion. She bumped into chairs, tables, and walls. She then ran into the familiar sofa and hit it with a *THUD!* Sage jumped up onto the sofa and began to dig at it with her paws, trying to make a hole to hide in or dig her way out of the house. She wanted to get away from the loud machine noises and from the strange voices.

About five minutes later, the loud pounding and drilling stopped. Sage listened intently.

"I think that telephone wire is fixed now," one of the men said to the other.

"It really needed to be replaced. That wiring was a mess!" the other man commented.

The strangers' voices became muffled as they walked away. Sage continued to listen with alert ears, and when she no longer heard the unfamiliar sounds, she lay down exhausted then slept.

A few hours later, the man and woman came home and found Sage lying near the back door. They also saw the tattered sofa cushions, torn by Sage's digging claws. They scolded the dog, and she hung her head in sorrow. Sage wished she could tell them how scared she had been, but she couldn't speak 'human.'

Several days passed, and although her people took good care of her, Sage felt unhappy and frightened. She continued to have a hard time getting around the house. She fell on the porch stairs. She bumped into walls, chairs, and tables. She also bumped into the man and woman. Sage's people noticed her struggles.

One afternoon Sage heard the woman say, "Even though her shots aren't due for another month, I think we should take Sage to the doctor."

Two days later the woman took Sage to the pet doctor, known as a veterinarian. He talked softly to her and petted her gently. He gave her two shots and shined a bright light into her eyes. Sage didn't blink or flinch. In fact, she hardly noticed the light.

Sage heard the veterinarian quietly say to the woman, "See how cloudy her eyes are," as he gently but firmly held Sage's head. "I suspect she's had this disease since birth. I'm sorry, but there's nothing we can do. Although I believe she can see a bit of light and shadow now, she'll soon be completely blind."

The woman cried a little, then she asked the doctor, "Why didn't her other owners tell us?"

"I don't know for sure, but there is a chance they didn't know," the doctor replied. "If she grew up in one place, she could have become familiar with where things were. She seems to have a great sense of hearing and a very good sense of smell. She's also very smart, as you well know. She may have been able to get around just fine at her other home. Then again, some people simply don't pay close attention to their pets."

The woman hugged Sage tightly, and Sage could feel her sorrow. The young dog rested her head on the woman's shoulder to comfort her; she did not like sensing people were sad. For a moment, the dog forgot her own fears and sadness. She wanted to help the lady be happy again. After all, isn't that part of a dog's job, to make a human's life happier? Sage nuzzled her head into the woman's hand.

"I'm so sorry, Sage," the lady whispered into the dog's ear. "I should have known something was terribly wrong when you were afraid of the stairs and when you bumped into the walls and the chairs. I never thought blindness. No wonder you were afraid!"

A sigh escaped from the woman's lips. "I wish there was something we could do for you," she said. "All we can really do is love you and take good care of you."

Sage felt the woman's hug tighten. "That is what you need anyway, isn't it, girl? Well, that's exactly what we're going to do!"

The strong sound in the woman's voice gave Sage greater comfort. She wagged her tail briskly. She felt the woman smile against her fur.

"Good girl," the woman said. "Let's go home. We need to do a few things to make life a little easier for you."

The woman led Sage, with leash on her collar, to the car and drove home.

Awhile later, at home, Sage sat on the floor next to the lady as the woman spoke with her husband. She felt the man's hand gently on her head. Sage sensed he was sad, too. She didn't like knowing these people were unhappy.

Sage also began to sense a calming Spirit deep within. She tipped her head and listened with her heart. She recognized this Whisper as the Great Creator and she listened as He reminded her how kindly these people treated her. They fed her well, played tug-of-war with her, and let her sit next to them on the newly repaired sofa. They talked gently to her and gave her special treats. At that moment, Sage realized these people were her family, that they loved her and that she loved them.

The Whisper instilled within the blind dog not to let fear guide her life and a way to do that would be to learn more about her new home. Sage resolved within herself to do just that.

She wagged her tail hard as her determination increased, thumping out a *Whack! Whack!* rhythm,. Hearing the sound of her tail beating strongly on the floor further sparked Sage's courage and love.

Sage nuzzled the man's face gently and licked his cheek. She sensed the lady bending down and putting her arms around her husband and then around Sage. The young dog felt content and safe within her people's tender and loving hug.

Later that evening the man bought a big plastic box that he set on the bedroom floor. He called for Sage, and she eagerly came to him, listening as his voice guided her down the hall and through the room. When she felt his hand on her back, Sage stopped. She sniffed the plastic box; it had the man's scent, and she immediately felt comfortable. She listened as the man said, "This is your kennel, a place for you to sleep, Sage. The kennel will also be a place you can go when you're frightened. Go inside now and check it out."

Sage heard the man snap his fingers, and she followed the snapping sound inside the plastic box. It was large, so large in fact, that when she sat upright, her head did not touch the top. She also still had room to wag her tail, which she did with great excitement! Her feet felt a soft, warm blanket on the kennel's floor. This must be a special place, Sage thought.

There it was again—that gentle, peaceful Whisper. Sage quieted herself and listened. She heeded the Whisper and lay down on the blanket. She realized the kennel, as well as this house, was a place of safety.

Sage closed her eyes and relaxed. That night she slept more soundly and more peacefully than she had in a long, long time.

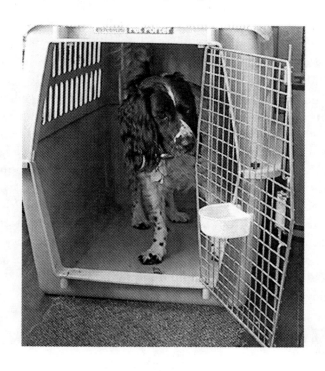

CHAPTER 4

Learning and Adapting

During the next several days Sage carefully explored her new surroundings. This house was now her home and she needed to learn how to manage in her state of blindness.

She walked through the rooms inside the house, learning where the chairs were by counting the number of dog steps between each rug in that room. She learned where the sofa, dining chairs and recliner chairs were located in the living room. By allowing her fur to brush the side of the walls, she made her way slowly down the hall to the bathroom and the bedrooms. She also learned the placement of the kitchen this way.

The kennel became her special spot; she felt safe and comfortable in the large box. She had chew toys inside and plenty of room to stretch out and sleep. She also slept on the floor, on the sofa, and on the bed—it was her choice. She had learned how to judge the height of pieces of furniture by resting her chin on them and then jumping up.

Sage enjoyed each resting area for she knew this was her home.

The large backyard even became less of a challenge for the blind dog. Sage walked the fence-line, memorizing where the bushes and small trees stood. She learned how many paces it took to reach the big tree from the back door, how many it took from the big tree to the fence, and from the tree to the bushes near the fence corners.

Sage explored slowly and intently. She found by slowing down she could hear and smell better, and she avoided head-on crashes with the large cottonwood tree even though it grew in the middle of the yard.

Within a few weeks, Sage became more familiar with her surroundings, and as she became more familiar, she became more confident in herself and trusting of her new family.

Sage learned to sense and listen to the Great Creator when the Whisper came to her inner self. The Whisper guided her as she explored the house and the yard, and comforted her when she rested. She realized this inner spirit was strong, loving and truthful.

As her confidence increased and her fears lessened, Sage began to play more outdoors. The spring days were getting longer and the sun was shining brighter and warmer. The backyard soon became her favorite place to spend the day. Sage could jump near the big tree with little trouble, and she did this often, especially when she heard or smelled the squirrels that lived and played in the branches. She ran after blue jays and red finches when they flew overhead, and she ran along the fence barking at other animals that roamed

by, such as cats and other dogs. Deer lived in the area, and Sage barked at them when she smelled them walk by the yard. She even came nose to nose with one, and Sage let it know that it was not welcome to come any closer. After all, it's a dog's job to protect her family's yard!

The squirrels were her favorite animals to chase. They reminded Sage of the rabbits at her former home. These little gray creatures enjoyed teasing Sage from the trees; she became very aware of them whenever they came near. She heard them jumping in the tree branches, running across the fence, and dashing through the grass. Her ears and her nose followed them throughout the yard, but, like the rabbits before them, Sage was not able to catch one. But, oh, how she did try!

One bushy-tail in particular seemed to delight in the game of 'tease the dog'. This critter taunted her unmercifully. It chattered from the tree branches just above her head and came within nose-length but then quickly darted

away. Sage trailed the squirrel as it ran from one end of the wooden fence to the other. After a few rounds of 'catch-me-if-you-can,' Sage laid on the back step and dreamt of one day catching that talkative tree dweller!

Sage also created special resting places in the yard. She spent time lying under the blooming lilac bush and dozing on the concrete porch in the sun. She also dug a hole near the edge of the house. When the sun became too warm on the porch, Sage lay in the hole to cool off. Sometimes she raised her head to sniff the air. After making sure nothing strange lurked about, she curled back up and slept.

The backyard wasn't her only outdoor entertainment. Sage traveled to many areas with her people, and as the weather turned warmer, the three friends frequently visited the mountains.

Spring in the Rocky Mountains is a refreshing, beautiful time of the year. Wildflowers and green meadows glisten against the white snow pack, and bluebirds, stellar jays, and mountain chickadees begin to nest. Sage and her family trekked to the Bighorns and the Snowy Range of Wyoming as well as the Beartooth and Absaroka Mountains of Montana. Alive with white phlox, purple violets, yellow glacier lilies, and countless birds and bumblebees, the mountains sprang to life beneath the feet of Sage and her friends, and the young dog sensed the season's energy and beauty.

These outings required Sage and her family to travel by car, sometimes a few hours, sometimes several. Some of their journeys took many days and required sleeping away from home. They over-nighted in a tent or a camp trailer, depending upon the weather. Sage's first experience sleeping in a tent was uncomfortable to say the least; even her people had a rough night's sleep on the ground!

However, the dog soon thrilled with these new adventures. She learned to create a nest of her own with the blankets given her to sleep on. And, *AH!* the crisp, clean air was simply delicious! She delighted in its freshness as well as in the many trails she walked with her family and in the cool mountain waters they discovered.

Many different fragrances came to her on these journeys, and Sage could hardly imagine all the many creatures and creations that left these scents. She enjoyed smelling each one!

CHAPTER 5

The Pet Store

Sage's first several months with her new family were filled with many new experiences. In addition to car rides, camping, and hiking, Sage's family took her other places, too.

One day as Sage lay on the back porch warming herself in the spring sun, the man stepped out of the house and said, "We're going for a car ride, Sage. Do you want to go?"

Sage had learned many words quickly, and 'car ride' had become a favorite—she knew what it meant. The man and woman sometimes left a window slightly rolled down so Sage could feel the wind blow through her ears and on her face. She hoped this would be one of those fun rides!

She immediately sat up and wagged her tail with excitement.

"We're going to a new pet store, Sage," the woman said. "This store allows pets to come inside and pick out treats, toys and food! This is going to be so much fun!"

The man laughed at his wife's enthusiasm.

"Maybe we should bring the camera," she added.

"Let's wait until next time for that," the man replied as he chuckled again.

After a short ride in the car, Sage walked between the couple through the parking lot with her head held high. Although she did not quite understand where they were going, hearing the excitement in their voices made Sage eager, too. She quickened her pace—she wanted to know what was so special about this place.

The sound of the store doors opening with a *WHOOSH* caused Sage to step back quickly. However, her people reassured her, and after she felt another gentle tug on her leash, Sage followed them into the store.

At once, her nose picked up many scents—other animals, other people, and aromas of treats and food. There were so many smells, Sage didn't know which direction to follow. But she did know one thing: this was a *great* place to be!

Within a short time, her keen nose picked up a scent more enticing than the others. She pulled on her leash and wagged her tail, eager to find that special fragrance.

The man tightened the leash slightly and said sternly, "Listen to us, Sage. We want you to be a good girl. This is going to be a new experience for all of us."

Although she tried to be obedient, Sage found it difficult to concentrate closely on her people's commands. There were many distractions, and Sage struggled to listen to and follow her people.

Sage quickened her pace. There it was again—that enticing aroma! The man and woman laughed and let Sage lead them to what interested her. She stopped near a shelf where the scent was strongest—the smell was like bacon and cheese. Oh, that would be *so good* to eat!

"You seem to like this one, Sage," the woman said as she knelt by the sharp-nosed dog. "We'll get you a few of these."

The three friends spent the next hour going up and down aisles. They found toys and treats, food and friends. Although Sage was often hesitant meeting up with other dogs because she couldn't see them, she barely flinched when a few dogs walked near. She stayed close to her people, and since they weren't upset Sage tried to not be anxious either. The entire store seemed filled with happy people and happy pets.

"This is quite an adventure, isn't it, Sage?" the woman said.

"I think our little friend is bound for many adventures in her life," the husband replied.

Sage wagged her tail in agreement.

As they walked out of the store with four sacks of dog goodies and toys, the man said to his wife, "I think you had as much fun as the dog!"

"I did!" she responded. "It's great to be able to take our little blind dog to the store and have her show us what she likes!"

"This store certainly brings out the pets and their owners," the man commented. "Did you see that lady with the cat in her shopping cart? It was lying in a basket and seemed as content as a clam in the ocean."

"Whoever thought of a store that allows pets and pet owners to shop together certainly had a wonderful idea," his wife added.

She bent down and rubbed Sage's back and head. "You did great, girl! What a smart, good dog you are! It's fun to shop for toys and treats for you! I promise you that we'll come back here again!"

Sage looked up with love in her eyes, and she wagged her tail in gratitude and anticipation.

That evening, Sage lay on the living room floor chewing on a new rawhide stick her people had purchased for her at the pet store. The man and woman sat next to each other on the sofa watching television. Sage had often heard the television and had adjusted to its many voices and noises. Suddenly, she stopped chewing and perked up her ears. What was that sound?

The noise came again, loud honking of Canada geese, and they sounded as though they were in the room. Sage quickly stood up, cocked her head and listened again. More honking! Sage walked first to the back door then to the front door. The honking faded. She walked back to the living room, and as she did, the geese honked again. The sounds were coming from the television!

Sage walked closer to the television, sat down and listened. Then she moved her head around the room, listening with intent ears. How could she catch those birds? After all, it's a Springer Spaniel's job to bring birds to her family!

She heard her people chuckle. "What is that, Sage?" the woman asked. "Do you hear those geese?"

"I think she'd try to catch them if they flew into the living room," her husband said with a laugh.

"Oh, I've no doubt! Hey, honey, I think Sage likes the Outdoor Channel!" the woman said.

"Yes she does, both the real outdoor channel and the one on television."

As the honking geese faded, new birds could be heard, including a bald eagle and a great horned owl. The various birdcalls intrigued Sage. She sat down near the TV and, although she could not see the pictures, she listened and enjoyed the many sounds of nature it produced.

"Come here, Sage," the woman coaxed, "come sit with us and listen to the TV."

Sage jumped up on the sofa and sat between her people, listening carefully just in case any of those birds actually came into the house. She was ready for them!

CHAPTER 6

More New Adventures

Summer arrived, and Sage and her family continued to enjoy each other's company. They traveled even more frequently, and during one those trips Sage stayed in a motel for the first time.

This first experience was scary for the young blind dog. The numerous strange voices and noises distressed her. The room in which she and her family stayed was located on the sixth floor, and they had to ride an elevator to reach it. She did not like the ride on this invention; it made her a bit motion sick. Her people encouraged and praised her, and she sat as close to them as she could. Feeling them next to her gave Sage comfort.

Learning to climb up and down the strange stairway also gave Sage concern. However, with the continuous encouragement from her people, she managed well.

Their next stay at a motel was less nerve-wracking for her, and upon their third trip she felt more relaxed. As long as her people were nearby or she lay in her kennel, Sage felt safe. She sat quietly on the elevator rides and managed the stairs carefully. She even became accustomed to hearing strange human voices, realizing those voices were not in the same room with her.

In order to help her become more comfortable with people and other animals, the man and woman often walked her through parks in the towns they visited. There Sage encountered other people and other pets, and through these interactions, Sage came to appreciate when people spoke to her and petted her. She came to understand most people were kind and affectionate and that other dogs could be good playmates. She especially liked the smaller dogs. She came to realize she had little to fear from them because, although she was blind, they respected her and enjoyed her playfulness. She often played and wrestled with these little ones. Sage made new friends, both human and animal, while visiting new places.

Although she enjoyed traveling with her people, Sage liked the comfort of home best of all. As the days grew longer and warmer, she spent a lot of time in the backyard. But Sage also found quiet times indoors with her people pleasant, too. In the evenings she either sat between the couple on the sofa or lay at their feet on a big, soft rug. Sometimes she chewed her rawhide bones, and sometimes she simply lay in quiet contentment.

The mornings were pleasant as well. Every day before breakfast, Sage's people rubbed her skin in really great ways, scratching her chin and her tummy. They rolled and wrestled on the floor and even set up a long tunnel in which she found biscuits and other treats. There were also games both of tug-of-war with her favorite rope and hide-the-squeaky-toy. At first Sage was startled by the sound, but when she discovered it came from a soft fuzzy toy and not something that could harm her, she had fun looking for it. She pretended the toy was a squirrel and that she was the mighty hunting dog determined to find it. Hide-and-seek-the-squeaky became a great indoor game to play!

Sage and her people spent time every day taking walks around the neighborhood. She was fearful to stroll along the streets at first because of the traffic, car horns, strangers' voices, and other dogs barking. However, Sage quickly became familiar with the route chosen by her people, and she listened closely to what they said.

She learned commands they repeated, including 'step-up,' 'step-down,' 'back' and 'stop.' Those instructions helped her navigate curbs, stairs and other things that might make their walk difficult. Her people praised her when she learned new things, and they gave her excited yet gentle pats of encouragement. Eager to hear their happy voices and feel their reassuring touches, Sage quickly learned these and many other words.

Within a short time, she instinctively knew where the street crossings took place, when to turn right, when to turn left, and how many steps from the step down curb to the step up one. She felt pride in mastering the walking course.

Summer progressed, and walks with her friends became a big highlight of Sage's day. Most walks occurred in the morning, and on warm, pleasant evenings a second daily walk might take place. Sage listened for the signals, such as shoes being put on her humans' feet and the dog leash being removed from its hook in the hallway. She wiggled joyfully when the leash was snapped to her collar. There were walks along the town streets and walks in the park, but there was one special place Sage most enjoyed traveling.

A nature trail was located near her home, and Sage liked walking this area best. Not only was she away from the street and its numerous noises, but sometimes she was allowed to wade in the creek which flowed nearby. The water felt refreshing on her skin, and she could easily walk along the creek's sandy bottom. Mid-summer was the best time at the creek because the water had not yet dried up nor was it too deep for a blind dog to wade in safely. There was often activity around the creek, mostly by other dogs and their people, and many times Sage's nose picked up the scent of a duck, a songbird or even a raccoon that had recently been at the water's edge.

After wading, Sage would shake the water from her body with vigor. Sometimes she sprayed other dogs or even people. She always had a good excuse though—she couldn't see them!

The trail winding around the creek was simply a dirt path. Located in town, this area served as open space, a place in a neighborhood that was left to nature. The open space provided a home for many types of wildlife, including deer, raccoons, skunks, ducks and lots of songbirds. Sage was glad her home was located nearby; it was quieter here than walking other places in town and closer to home than the outings to the mountains.

After a refreshing outdoor bath in the creek, Sage walked with her people along the dirt trail. Throughout the entire circle route, she could smell many different creatures, including mice, deer, squirrels, and rabbits. The open space might be located in town, but here the animals could live freely and securely. Sage enjoyed stopping along the way and smelling the wild animals that had walked on or near the trail, too.

Sometimes along the journey she encountered other people with their dogs. Although most were polite, some dogs wanted to get in her face. Sage didn't like that, and she was not shy about letting them know!

During one morning walk on the trail, her nose detected an animal scent she did not know. The smell was strong and unpleasant, and Sage barked several times with alarm. She wasn't sure she wanted to meet this animal her people called 'a black bear'—the smell was worse than a wet dog! She hoped she would never encounter that smell again!

CHAPTER 7

Additions to the Family

August arrived and the heat was tremendous. Sage stayed outdoors most mornings, but her people insisted she stay inside during the hot afternoon. Sometimes Sage wished she could tell them she wanted to be outside, lying in her cool dirt hole which she had dug near the house. Her hole felt as good to her if not better than the air conditioning inside the house.

On one of those hot August afternoons, the lady came home early from work. Sage greeted her at the front door as usual, but something wasn't quite right: there was a new smell to the lady. Sage sniffed and sniffed, trying to discover what that smell was. The woman chuckled and said, "I have a surprise for you, Sage. We have two new friends coming to live with us."

Sage now detected the new smell: cats! She had smelled cats before outside but never this close or in this house, *HER* house! She wasn't sure she liked this idea.

Sage heard a small door open then close. The cat smell became more intense as two young kittens crept out of a cat carrier. They each arched their backs and hissed at Sage.

"Now, Bailey and Murphy, you need to be nice to Sage, and Sage, you need to welcome these little ones," the woman said. "I know it will take some time, but we're all family here."

Sage again sniffed around and she heard the young cats hiss again at her and then race away down the hall. How could she make friends if they ran off like that? She wasn't sure she wanted to become friends with a cat anyway, let alone *TWO* cats!

This would take getting used to for all of them.

The kitties spent that first night in a room of their own while Sage slept in her kennel in the bedroom as she normally did. But, there was nothing normal about this night. The fact there were cats in her house kept Sage awake, and often she raised her head to listen as the little sisters meowed and walked around restlessly in the other room. Her people did not get much sleep that night either.

The next morning the kitties had the run of the house while the humans went to work and Sage stayed in the backyard. Ever the protector of her family's house, she kept an ear to the door to hear what might be happening inside. What were those little critters up to? Would they go into her kennel? It was bad enough the whole house now had the scent of cat—Sage didn't want her kennel smelling of kitty, too!

Meanwhile, the kittens carefully investigated each room and closet. When they came to Sage's kennel, they sniffed at it then arched their backs, hissed, and slowly backed away. *That dog smell!*

After scouting out the house and some time chasing fuzzy fake mice, the kitties curled up on a chair for a quick nap. But, it was just a short one—although Murphy and Bailey knew Sage was in the backyard, they didn't know when she would come into the house!

That afternoon the woman stayed home from work and kept Sage in the house. The August sun heated the day to nearly 95 degrees, too hot for Sage to stay outside, the woman said. She shut the door to the backroom and to her bedroom so the kitties could not hide or stay to themselves. She tried to entice them to play with string, and it occupied their young minds for a few minutes, but, when Sage heard them playing, she came to inspect. When the kitties saw her, they hissed, arched their backs and scampered down the hall to the bathroom.

This might be fun after all, Sage thought. These cats could be her indoor squirrels!

The lady allowed that to happen only once then she scolded Sage. "The kitties are part of our house now, Sage. They are not toys or squirrels to play with."

Sage lay down quietly on the living room rug and tried to ignore the kittens. She listened as Murphy, the longhaired black and white kitty, cautiously approached. Sage lay perfectly still and allowed the kitten to sniff her face. The kitty's whiskers tickled Sage's nose; the young dog sneezed. With a frightened hiss, the kitten raced away.

Sage sighed. She hadn't meant to scare the little cat. Living with cats *WILL BE* a challenge, she thought.

That evening, as Sage lay with a chew toy on the living room rug, her senses detected the two sisters in the room. Both carefully approached and began to sniff from the bottom of Sage's tail all the way to her head. Sage lay still and let the kitties smell her completely. The man and woman sat in their recliner chairs. The woman called to her husband softly, "Dear, look."

He glanced over and saw the kitties examining the young dog.

"Interesting," he commented.

"Do you think they understand Sage is blind?"

"If not, they will soon enough," the husband replied.

Sage stopped chewing and lay with her head on her paws. A gentle, mothering instinct began to build within her. In some ways, the kittens were like she had been many months earlier, moving to a new home and having to leave behind all that was familiar.

Sage soon felt one of the kittens lie down next to her. It was Murphy, the longhaired black and white. The woman commented to her husband, "Look, honey, our two black and white pets have become friends."

Within a few weeks, all three pets were comfortable with each other. Murphy and Sage often slept together on the sofa, and Bailey, the three-colored, shorthaired sister, accepted Sage as a playmate. She created a game with the blind dog—a game of tag. Bailey would touch Sage's nose then quickly run off; Sage used her keen sense of smell to sniff out Bailey's location, touch the kitten's nose, and the game would start again.

The kitties adopted Sage's tail as a toy. Despite her blindness, Sage was a happy dog and her tail often reflected her attitude; rarely did it stop wagging. When Sage laid on the sofa or the bed, the kittens often played with the fringe-like fur on her tail. Sage tolerated this play for a time, but let the kitties know when enough was enough.

During the mornings while Sage was outside, the kitties played with their many toys, including furry fake mice and scrunch balls. They also had a carpeted tower to climb, which they often did. When they sat on the top, they could look out the big picture window into the backyard. They watched as Sage patrolled the fence line or chased the squirrels. They also noticed with great interest when the songbirds came to the outdoor bird feeders. There were gray juncos, black-capped chickadees, rosy red finches and brown flickers with red on their heads. Bailey and Murphy watched the birds fly from the bushes to the feeders and back again. Their little kitty tails swished back and forth.

Maybe one day they would be old enough and strong enough to be outside, too. For now, though, they were content to observe the outside from the safety of being inside. They knew, too, that later in the day, their friend Sage would be back inside to spend time with them.

Sage realized the kitties were just inside the door. She sensed another presence, too, from deep within herself. She had felt this before, and she had learned to listen to the calm, reassuring Whisper of the Great Creator. As she remained quiet within, she sensed the Whisper tell her that, although blind, she had a great purpose, a great responsibility. She not only had her people to love and protect, now there were young ones to watch over and care for as well.

Sage straightened her shoulders and sat up straight. She would fulfill her dog duties and be a companion for her people and the kitties.

CHAPTER 8

Lost!

One warm early September afternoon, Sage and her people left the house and took a two-hour car ride. Sage felt the car stop after several miles along a gravel road. The man helped her out of the car, leading her out by her leash.

Sage could tell they were in a forested area, and although she and her people had visited many forested and mountainous areas this year, the place they were visiting now was unfamiliar. Sage walked carefully through the woods, feeling pine needles, pinecones and small rocks under her feet. She listened for her humans' footsteps and gentle voices and followed them.

Sage felt the grass and dirt under her paws and smelled evergreen trees and fresh air. She wondered where they were and where they were going. Soon she heard the sound of rushing water, louder than the creek near her home.

"There's a river here, Sage," the man told her. "I know you enjoy the creek, but this is bigger and faster. You can go in, but we're going to keep the leash on so you'll be safe."

Sage stepped carefully near the river. She knew about water—she had been bathed many times in the bathtub and she liked wading in the creek near her home. She could tell, however, this was different. It sounded bigger.

Sage took a few more cautious steps. Soon her paws felt wet. She walked out farther. She felt the water rise to the top of her legs. Although she stumbled a bit on the rocks, the calm voices of her people reassured her. She walked around a bit more and soon the water rose above Sage's belly. She stretched out her front legs and then Sage began to swim.

This was fun! The water was nearly to her shoulders and it felt cool as the summer sun warmed her back. Although she couldn't see where she was going, she trusted the man who held her leash. Sometimes she felt a tug, and she turned in the direction the man was guiding her. Sage continued to splash and swim, and she heard laughter coming from her people as they watched and waited for her on the river shore.

Sage took a swim break when she felt the water get lower on her body. She walked when her feet touched the river's rocky bottom and she waded around a bit. Then she returned to the deeper water and swam some more. Sage spent 20 minutes in the water, swimming and wading. Then she heard the man call, "Come, Sage" as he tugged gently on her leash.

The young dog stepped from the water, knowing the man still held her leash securely. She paused at the water's edge, stood completely still for a moment, and listened to the wind as it whispered in the trees. She felt another Whisper as well and Sage felt strong and confident. Her eyesight was completely gone, but she knew deep within herself that she could still do many things other dogs enjoy—like playing, exploring, walking, even swimming. Sage shook herself and stood proudly, tail and head held high.

She heard the man call her name again, and she followed the sound of his voice until she stood next to him. She paused momentarily and then mischievously shook the water from her body, spraying the man and his wife like a shower. The two humans laughed and patted her head.

"Let's go for a walk then have a picnic before we head home," the woman suggested.

"Good idea," her husband replied. "Come on, Sage."

The three friends walked through the forest for a few moments then came to a meadow filled with grass and wildflowers. Although Sage could not see the reds, blues and yellows splashed across the grassy canvas, deep inside she knew this was a special place. Sage let out a joyous bark, and her friends laughed happily.

"It is a wonderful day, isn't it, Sage?" the woman said.

Sage's tail wagged vigorously in response.

Soon they came to the area near where the car was parked. This was a picnicking area, complete with green wooden tables, cast-iron grills, and large metal garbage cans. As Sage's people sat at a table eating their sandwiches, the dog's ears remained on alert for any sound. Besides the rushing river a half-mile away, Sage's keen sense of hearing picked up the small sounds of chirping songbirds and the rustle of aspen leaves.

Sage cocked her head to listen more closely. Was that a squirrel? Sage's ears listened more intently. Sure enough, off in the distance, she heard the faint yet distinct sound of a chattering squirrel.

Sage began to walk away from the picnic area. Her people were packing the picnic items into the car and didn't notice her wandering from them. Sage blocked out all other sounds and smells in her intense search for the squirrel. She put her nose to the ground, picked up a strong scent, and quickly followed it to a tree. She raised her head as if to try to see the squirrel. She hadn't yet caught a squirrel in the backyard, but maybe she could catch one in the forest!

Soon Sage heard the chatter of yet another squirrel on a branch not far away. Excited, she began to run.

Her head hit a tree, which caused the squirrel to shriek with alarm. Sage heard this one jump from the branch to another tree, and, after shaking her head to clear the fogginess, Sage was again on her squirrel search. She was determined to not let this one get away.

It leaped from tree to tree, and Sage continued to follow. This one was probably leading her to an entire family of squirrels, Sage thought. She'd catch not just one, but *BUNCHES!* She continued to run through the forest.

Two hours passed. Sage grew weary of the game, for that's what these creatures seemed to be playing. The squirrels squawked but did not come out of the trees. Never once did Sage get close to even one of those pesky chattering squirrels.

Sage realized she was hungry. She turned to go back to the place where her people had been eating. Where were they anyway? She sniffed the air. She could not smell them. Her nose picked up only the fresh forest air and the many squirrels that lived in this woodland. She cocked her head to listen. Only the breeze spoke to her. Sage began to tremble for she realized she was lost.

Frightened, Sage tried to find her way through the forest. Her feet found a path and she walked. And walked. And walked some more. The path didn't seem to end. She picked up her own scent many times—she had been walking in a circle. Sage grew weary and even more frightened. She let out a mournful howl. Then, deep inside herself she felt the Whisper of the Great Creator guiding her to quietness. Sage listened to that Whisper, one she had heard within herself many times. She decided to lie down awhile.

Sage curled up under a tall pine tree but did not sleep. With her head on her paws, the young blind dog kept listening for a familiar voice. Maybe her people would find her. With that thought, after about 20 minutes, she fell into a fitful sleep.

She awoke to the smell of deer as they walked close by. Picking up Sage's scent, the two does quickly bounded away. Sage raised her head. Another time she would have followed those deer, but she needed to find her people. She stood up, put her nose to the ground and walked a few feet, trying to detect something familiar. With a few more steps her nose came across a scent that was familiar but one that she didn't want to smell. She had encountered this smell one other time on the trail near her home. It was the scent of that creature her people had called 'a black bear'.

The Whisper urged her to leave this spot quickly, and she did. If she could find the river, Sage might be able to follow the scent of her people. She wasn't sure where the river was because she wasn't sure of where she was. Once again came the Whisper from within, instructing her to continue walking straight. She listened, and after 15 more minutes of walking Sage heard the rushing river. Her pace quickened and she followed the river's calling.

New sounds came to the dog, the sound of human voices. Sage stopped and listened. Could they be her people? She couldn't be sure because of the loudness of the river. The voices grew closer. These were loud voices of strange men and they were coming closer. Sage panicked and began to run.

Her body crashed through bushes filled with stickers. These stickers stuck to her fur and a branch scratched her face. Sage barked in fear and frustration, and then she heard running footsteps. Sage shook herself loose from the sticker bushes and ran toward the river.

"I think that's her!" one of the men yelled.

Sage heard footsteps running near her. She jumped in the water and began to wade into the river.

"Wait!" the strange man said. "Stop, dog!"

"Sage!" another voice yelled.

The young dog paused. This voice had a familiar sound to it, but it was hard to be certain above the rush of the river. Then a woman's voice sounded out, but more softly.

"Sage, stop. Stop, Sage," the woman said.

Again the young blind dog heard the Great Creator's whisper so she paused and listened. She heard slight footsteps along the river's shore.

"Sage, it's all right," the woman's voice said.

Then another voice, a familiar man's voice, said firmly but quietly, "Sage, come."

Relief filled the dog as she recognized the voices of the man and the woman. Her people had found her!

The blind dog splashed gratefully through the water as she listened to the coaxing voices of the man and woman. When she reached the shore, she leaped for joy and felt them each grab her and hug her tightly.

"Oh, Sage!" the woman exclaimed, "I'm so glad we found you! You ran off so fast we couldn't keep up! We've been looking for you for hours!"

She heard more human footsteps walk up briskly then stop beside her people.

"I'm glad she's been found. A blind dog lost out here could have been a disaster," one of the strange men said.

"Yes, and thank you for your help," Sage's man replied. "If you hadn't been around . . ."

"Glad we could help. Remember to keep your dog on a leash and tied to something next time you're on a picnic."

"Yes, officer, you're right," the woman replied. "We just didn't think."

"Springers go after all sorts of things they hear and smell, it's just their nature," the sheriff replied. "I'm just glad this turned out all right."

"Believe me, so are we."

The sheriff bent down next to Sage. "Looks like she's got a bit of a gash on her face. You might have your vet look at that once you get home."

"Come on, Sage," the familiar male voice said. "Let's go home. We've all had a very big day."

With her leash securely on her collar, Sage followed her people back to the car. As they walked the dirt trail, Sage sniffed constantly, picking up the familiar scents along the way. She had been on the correct trail, but in her panic had passed the right turn and instead had been running in circles. Now, calmer, Sage discovered where she had made her mistake. She was thankful her people and others came looking for her; now she was safe and going home.

CHAPTER 9

It's Good to Be Home

The next evening at home, Sage sat in the backyard under the tall cottonwood tree. She had spent most of the day at the vet's office. The doctor cleaned the big cut on her face and the many scratches her body had received. The vet had also given her a bath. Sage felt refreshed and happy. She was home again! The kitties had sensed something happened when she and her family came home last night, and both sisters rubbed against Sage. They did the same when she returned from her visit to the pet doctor. She welcomed their comfort as much as she did the reassuring pats and hugs from her people.

Just as in the human world, life for a dog can be a big adventure, and Sage had experienced many in the past few months. The adventure of being lost though was one she didn't want to repeat.

She stared past the large cottonwood tree which grew in the middle of the yard. Its leaves were turning yellow. Like the leaves changing color, many changes had come Sage's way. Deep inside, she felt there would be more to come. Those changes, like adventures, would be both exciting and challenging, and they would be things to learn from.

Sage knew there were many things she had accomplished and many things yet for her to do. Blindness would not stop her from living life. She had a home and people to protect. But there would be fun times as well. She looked forward to the many walks she would take and many other adventures she would have with her people. She also looked forward to the many nights of lying either at their feet or next to them, cuddled and snuggled and bundled with love. Sage knew these people would forever give her a home and their attention and affection, just as she had given hers and always would. She also thought of Bailey and Murphy—she and the kitties were now good friends. It was a great feeling to have friends and to be loved!

There would also be times spent alone. Sage no longer feared being by herself. She was comfortable in the house as well as in the yard. She had playtime, she had quiet time, and she had a job to do. Sage barked at strange noises and voices, letting whoever or whatever was out there know that a dog now guarded this yard and this house. No one and nothing was going to get

past her! Who knows—maybe one day she'd even catch a pesky, chattering squirrel! She would, however, limit her squirrel chasing to the backyard.

The sun began to set. It looked like a fiery ball surrounded by apricot-colored cottony clouds. The sky gleamed in shades of blue, pink and yellow. She could not see the colors, but the Whisper inside herself told her that the evening was special and that she was special. Many days in her life had been unique. In fact, her entire life was a fascinating journey.

Sage walked a few steps and stared straight ahead for a moment. She listened carefully. There was very little sound; even the wind was still. As the sky's horizon filled with rainbow lights, fragrances of roses and honeysuckle mixed with other autumn scents and floated through the late evening air. She felt snug, both inside and out, as the setting sun bathed her with warmth.

She raised her head. Her lips drew back, and Sage smiled.

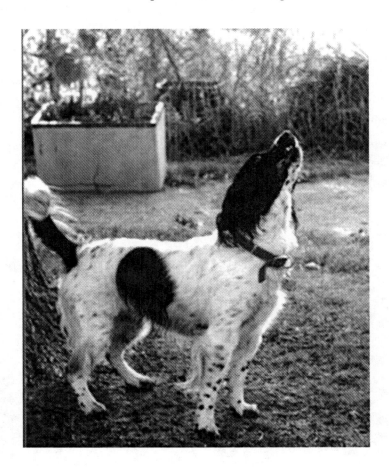

Meet Sage!

Sage is a real blind dog, and this is her story. She lives with Gayle and Greg Irwin in Wyoming. She has a disease called Progressive Retinal Degeneration, a disease of the eyes that causes dogs to go blind. It is hereditary. She was diagnosed at the age of 2 after the Irwins adopted her. Although she could see shadows at that time, it was not long before she completely lost her sight.

Sage has adapted very well to the loss of her eyesight. She uses her strong senses of smell and hearing as mentioned in this story. She learns very quickly and is a loving, intelligent and brave dog. Her tail rarely stops wagging and reflects her positive attitude. Her family dearly loves and respects her and is awed by her courage.

Sage has many friends, both human and animal. She lives a happy and healthy life thanks to her family, her friends, and her vet Dr. Justin Johnson. If she could, Sage would say a **GREAT BIG THANK YOU** to each one. Sage and her family hope her story inspires readers and gives hope and courage to all.